Living with Light

Nicola Baxter

CHILDRENS PRESS ®

CHICAGO

What can you see when it is almost dark?

We need light to see colors and shapes. What would the world be like if there was no light?

The sun is a glowing ball of gases
a long way off in space.

Here on Earth we see the light
and feel the heat
of this giant glowing ball.

5

The sun is so bright that it can light up
Earth even when there are clouds
in front of it.
Never look straight at the sun.
It could hurt your eyes.

Sometimes the light from the sun
seems too bright.
We can't see well because we're dazzled.

7

Every day the sun moves across the sky.
In the evening, it seems to disappear.
It is hidden behind Earth until morning.
While the sun is hidden, it is dark.

Try this...
Draw a picture of your school and show where the sun
is in the middle of the day.

8

When the sun is not shining,
we can turn on other kinds of lights.
Most lights use electricity to
make them work.

Some electric lights are very bright.

Light can shine through glass or
clear plastic.
We say these things are transparent.
That means we can see through them.

How many things can you think of
that are made of glass or clear plastic?

Light cannot shine through most things.
When something blocks out sunlight,
it makes a dark shape.
This dark shape is called a shadow.

Try this...

Shine a bright light on the wall.
Then put your hands in front of the light
and make shadow shapes.

15

At night there is not much light.

Some animals sleep in the daytime and come out when it is dark.

At night, their eyes can see in the dark better than our eyes can.

Our eyes need light to see properly. The light goes into our eyes through the small black circle in the middle. It is called the pupil.

Try this...

Look at a bright light for two minutes. Then look in a
mirror. What size are your pupils? Now put your hands
over your eyes for two minutes. Then look at your
pupils again. Are they bigger or smaller?
Your pupils get bigger to let in more light.

Lights can help us notice things, especially in the dark.
They can be used just for fun...

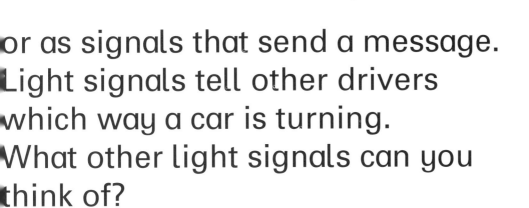

or as signals that send a message.
Light signals tell other drivers
which way a car is turning.
What other light signals can you
think of?

Nothing can live without light.
Green plants make their own food using light from the sun.
Insects and animals eat the plants.
People eat some of the
plants and animals.
Without light from the sun,
there would be nothing on Earth to eat!

Index

1996 Childrens Press Edition

© 1995 Watts Books
All rights reserved
Published simultaneously in
Canada

1 2 3 4 5 6 7 8 9 10 00 99 98 97 96

Editor: Sarah Ridley

Designer: Nina Kingsbury

Illustrator: Michael Evans

Library of Congress Cataloging in Publication Data

Baxter, Nicola.
   Living with light / by Nicola Baxter; illustrated
by Michael Evans.
      p. cm. — (Toppers)
   ISBN 0-516-09268-5
   1. Light—Juvenile literature. 2. Light—
Experiments—juvenile literature. [1. Light. 2.
Light—Experiments. 3. Experiments.] I. Evans,
Michael, 1966- ill. II. Title. III. Series: Baxter,
Nicola. Toppers.
QC360.B39 1995   94-44724
535—dc20   CIP AC

The publishers would like to thank
Carol Olivier, Jason Botross and
Leanne Bates of Kenmont Primary
School for their help with this
book.

Photographs: Bruce Coleman Ltd
17; Eye Ubiquitous 11; Robert
Harding Picture Library 5, 9, 14, 20;
Hutchison Library 6; Peter Millard
cover, 2, 3, 18; Natural History
Photographic Agency 23; Oxford
Scientific Films 12.

Printed in Malaysia